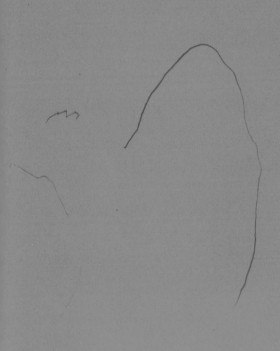

Cowgirl Kate and Cocoa

Cowgirl Kate and Cocoa

Written by **Erica Silverman**

Painted by **Betsy Lewin**

Harcourt, Inc.

Orlando   Austin   New York   San Diego   London

To Julia, the newest Torn—E. S.
To horses everywhere—B. L.

Text copyright © 2005 by Erica Silverman
Illustrations copyright © 2005 by Betsy Lewin

For information about permission to reproduce selections from this book,
please write Permissions, Houghton Mifflin Harcourt Publishing Company,
215 Park Avenue South, NY, NY 10003.

www.hmhbooks.com

First Harcourt paperback edition 2006

The Library of Congress has cataloged the hardcover edition as follows:
Silverman, Erica.
Cowgirl Kate and Cocoa/Erica Silverman; illustrated by Betsy Lewin.
p. cm.
Summary: Cowgirl Kate and her cowhorse, Cocoa, who is always hungry, count cows,
share a story, and help each other fall asleep.
[1. Cowgirls—Fiction. 2. Horses—Fiction.]
I. Lewin, Betsy, ill. II. Title.
PZ7.S58625Co 2005
[E]—dc22 2004005739
ISBN-13: 978-0152-02124-5 ISBN-10: 0-15-202124-8
ISBN-13: 978-0152-05660-5 pb ISBN-10: 0-15-205660-2 pb

SCP   20 19 18 17 16

4500444293

Printed in China

The illustrations in this book were done in watercolors on
Strathmore one-ply Bristol paper.
The display type was hand lettered by Georgia Deaver.
The text type was set in Filosofia Regular.
Color separations by Bright Arts Ltd., Hong Kong
Printed and bound by RR Donnelley, China
Production supervision by Pascha Gerlinger
Designed by Scott Piehl

Chapter 1
A Story for Cocoa

Cowgirl Kate rode her horse, Cocoa,
out to the pasture.
"It's time to herd cows," said Cowgirl Kate.
"I am thirsty," said Cocoa.
He stopped at the creek
and took a drink.

"Are you ready now?" asked Cowgirl Kate.

"No," said Cocoa. "Now I am hungry."

Cowgirl Kate gave him an apple.

He ate it in one bite.

Then he sniffed the saddlebag.

Cowgirl Kate gave him another apple.

He ate that in one bite, too.

He sniffed the saddlebag again.

"You are a pig," said Cowgirl Kate.

"No," said Cocoa. "I am a horse."

"A cowhorse?" she asked.

"Of course," he said.

"But a cowhorse herds cows," she said.

"Just now, I am too full," he said.

Cowgirl Kate smiled.

"Then I will tell you a story."

"Once there was a cowgirl
who needed a cowhorse.
She went to a ranch and
saw lots and lots of horses.
Then she saw a horse
whose coat was the color
of chocolate.
His tail and mane
were the color of caramel.
'Yum,' said the cowgirl,
'you are the colors
of my favorite candy.'
The horse looked at her.
He sniffed her."

"'Are you a real cowgirl?' he asked.
'I am a cowgirl from the
boots up,' she said.
'Well, I am a cowhorse from
the mane down,' he said.
'Will you work hard every day?' the cowgirl asked.
The horse raised his head high. 'Of course,' he said,
'a cowhorse always does his job.'
'At last,' said the cowgirl, 'I have found my horse.'"

"That was a good story," said Cocoa.

He raised his head high.

"And now I am ready to herd cows."

Chapter 2
The Surprise

One morning
Cowgirl Kate brought a box
to the barn.

"What is in that box?" Cocoa asked.

"A surprise," said Cowgirl Kate.

"Sugar cookies?" he asked.

"A surprise," she said.

"Apple pie?" he asked.

"A surprise," she said.

"Give me my surprise!" he said.

"First eat your oats," she said.

Cocoa glared at the bucket.

He kicked it over.

Cowgirl Kate frowned.

"That was your breakfast," she said.

Cocoa snorted.

"I am done with my breakfast," he said.

"I want my surprise."

"First I must groom you,"
said Cowgirl Kate.
She curried him.

She brushed him.

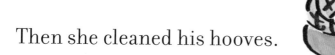
Then she cleaned his hooves.

Cocoa stomped.

"I want my surprise now!"

He pushed open the box.

He took a big bite
of the surprise.

He chewed.

He swallowed.

"Yuck!" he said.

"This does not taste
good at all!"

"Of course not," said Cowgirl Kate.
"It is a hat."
She put the hat on Cocoa's head
and held up a mirror.
"Do you like it?" she asked.

Cocoa frowned.

"I have only two ears," he said.

"But this hat has three holes!"

Cowgirl Kate laughed.

"Next time," she said,

"eat your breakfast

and not your surprise."

Chapter 3
Counting Cows

Cowgirl Kate was counting cows.

"Fifty-eight, fifty-nine—"

"There sure are a lot of cows," said Cocoa.

"Shhh!" said Cowgirl Kate.

"You are messing me up."

"I am hungry," said Cocoa.
"You are always hungry,"
said Cowgirl Kate.
Cocoa leaned down
and munched some grass.

Cowgirl Kate slid to the ground.

"I will count cows myself!" she said.

But she was too short.

She could not see all the cows.

She climbed up onto the fence,

but she still could not see all the cows.

She went to the tallest tree
and started to climb.
Up she went,
higher
and higher
and higher.
Cocoa galloped over.
"Come down, please!" he cried.
"I do not want you to fall."

"Don't worry," said Cowgirl Kate.

"I am a good climber."

"And *I* am a good worrier," said Cocoa.

"Please come down!

I will help you count cows."

Cowgirl Kate smiled.

She backed down the tree

and got into her saddle.

"Thank you," she said.

"Now I can see all the cows.

But I cannot remember

how many I counted."

"You counted fifty-nine," said Cocoa,
"and then I counted ten more."
Cowgirl Kate stared at him.
"But you were eating," she said.
"When did you do all that counting?"

Cocoa raised his head high.
"I am a talented cowhorse," he said.
"I can eat and count at the same time."

Chapter 4
Bedtime in the Barn

One night Cowgirl Kate slept in the barn.
"Good night, Cocoa," she said.
She crawled into her sleeping bag
and closed her eyes.

"Will you please fluff my straw?" Cocoa asked.

Cowgirl Kate sighed.

"I am very tired," she said.

But she climbed out of her sleeping bag
and fluffed his straw.
Then she crawled back into her sleeping bag.

"I am hungry," said Cocoa.

Cowgirl Kate sighed.

"You are always hungry," she said.

But she climbed out of her sleeping bag
and gave him three carrots.
Then she crawled back into her sleeping bag.

"Uh-oh! My water bin is low," said Cocoa.

Cowgirl Kate groaned.

"Why didn't you tell me that before?"

"I didn't think of it before," said Cocoa.

"First I was thinking about straw.

Then I was thinking about food.

Now I am thinking about water."

"You are doing too much thinking,"

said Cowgirl Kate.

But she climbed out of her sleeping bag
and filled up his water bin.

"Is there anything else?" she asked.

"No," said Cocoa.

"Good," she said.

"Now think about sleep!"

"Good night, Katie," said Cocoa.

"Good night, Cocoa," said Cowgirl Kate.

The barn was cold.
Cowgirl Kate pulled the sleeping bag
up to her chin.
The moon was bright.
She pulled the sleeping bag
over her eyes.

An owl hooted outside.

Whoooooo. Whoooooo.

Cowgirl Kate shivered.

"Cocoa! I cannot sleep," she said.

"Then I will sing you a lullaby," said Cocoa.

"Rock-a-bye, cowgirl,
on your cowhorse.
Though the wind blows,
you'll never be tossed.
When the dawn breaks,
your cowhorse will say,
'My hat's on. I'm ready
to herd cows all day.'"

And Cowgirl Kate smiled,
snuggled close...
and fell asleep.